I Know You Won't Forget

Story by
Truly Blessed Ink

Illustrations by
Carol Jordan

SQUARE CIRCLE PRESS

I Know You Won't Forget

Published by
Square Circle Press LLC
137 Ketcham Road
Voorheesville, New York 12186
www.squarecirclepress.com

First paperback edition.
ISBN-13: 978-0-9856926-2-9
ISBN-10: 0-9856926-2-6
Library of Congress Control Number: 2007901754
Printed and bound in the United States of America.

This book is dedicated to our Creator, our families, our friends, professionals, and survivors of TBI.

Without their love and support this book would not have been possible.

We hope this story brings understanding and hope to all who read it.

Truly Blessed Ink

Joey was a young boy who enjoyed playing baseball and soccer.

He lived with his mother and had to help her around the house while his father was away in the military.

One day, when Joey returned from baseball practice, he found out that his mom had been in an accident. She hurt her head badly and was taken to the hospital.

The doctors called it a BRAIN INJURY.

While his mom was in the hospital, Joey stayed with his aunt and uncle and visited her every day.

Joey was very happy when his mom finally went home.

He hoped that their life would return to normal, but something seemed to be different about his mom.

Because of her brain injury, Joey's mom forgot how to do some activities. She could not remember simple things like ...

the names of family members ...

how to tie her shoes ...

or how to do housework.

Joey felt sad that his mom had gotten hurt. Still, he wished things were like they were before the accident.

His mom got lost when driving, she was behind in her housework, and she sometimes forgot what she had promised to do.

Joey wished his mom was more like other kids' moms.

One time when Joey wanted to have a birthday party with his classmates, his mom promised to take cupcakes to his school for the party. Joey and his friends were excited.

His mom never showed up.

Joey was embarrassed and frustrated. He felt even worse when his classmates made fun of him. He yelled at some of them and got into trouble with the teacher.

Joey was still upset when he got home from school that day. He shouted, "How could you forget my birthday party?!"

Before she could answer, Joey screamed, "I hate you! I wish you weren't my mother!"

His mom began to cry.

Joey ran to his room and slammed the door.

The next day at school, Butch, the class bully, teased Joey about his mom.

The teacher had to break up the fight and made Joey stay after school to see a counselor.

The counselor told Joey that she was worried about him.

Joey told her about his mom's accident. He said he was scared because his mom wasn't the same.

The counselor told Joey that there was a way he could help his mom to remember important things. She taught Joey how to ...

make a list of THINGS TO DO ...

use a CALENDAR for appointments ...

put a STICKY NOTE in an important place ...

draw a PICTURE of something to do ...

use a TAPE RECORDER to remember conversations ...

and how to set an ALARM CLOCK.

The counselor made a list of these activities. She called them STRATEGIES.

The counselor warned Joey that some of the activities might not work for his mom.

"She needs to find out which ones help her the most," the counselor said. "It might take a while before your mom learns to use them."

Before Joey left, the counselor reminded him, "There is one thing the brain injury cannot change, and that is how much your mom loves you."

Joey was excited that he might be able to help his mom. When he got home, he told her about the strategies. They started using them right away.

After a few days, things seemed to be getting better, but there were still some problems.

Some ideas didn't work for his mom. Others did work, but she forgot to use them.

After a while, Joey's mom learned what worked best for her.

When she forgot something, Joey would remind her.
Joey and his mom were happy once again.

One day the new playground at school finally opened. Joey was excited to try out the new slide.

He told his mom he really wanted to stay after school to play with his friends.

Joey's mom gave him permission and said, "Have fun with your friends! I will pick you up on my way home from the grocery store."

Joey was worried that his mother would forget to pick him up. Before he left for school, he drew a picture of himself on the new slide. He gave it to his mom to help her remember to pick him up.

"I know you won't forget," Joey said. He watched as she put it next to her grocery list.

When the school day ended, Joey ran outside.
He wanted to be first on the new slide.

All the kids seemed to be having fun, but Joey
noticed that Butch was standing alone by the
trees. He looked unhappy.

Joey felt sorry he had fought with Butch. He walked over to him and asked if something was wrong. "No one ever wants to play with me," Butch replied sadly.

"Come on," Joey said, "you should try the new slide."

After playing on the slide, the two boys used the swings, the monkey bars, and the fire pole. They played all afternoon and had a lot of fun together.

It was getting late and Joey's mom still hadn't come. Most of the other kids had gone home. Joey was worried that she had forgotten to pick him up.

When Butch's mom came to pick him up, he asked her if they could wait until Joey's mom got there. It made Joey happy that they wanted to wait with him.

Suddenly, Joey's mom pulled into the parking lot.
He breathed a big sigh of relief.

Joey thanked Butch and his mom for waiting with him.
They made plans to stay after school again the next day.

As Joey scrambled into the car, he noticed his mom had taped the drawing right to the dashboard. She had used her strategy, and it worked perfectly!

She apologized for being late. "There was a long checkout line at the grocery store," she explained. Joey said, "I'm so proud you're my mom!" On their way home, he told his mom all about the playground and his new friend Butch.

What is a brain injury?

Your brain is a very important part of your body and is not like anyone else's brain. It makes you who you are – how you think, how you talk, how you act and how you feel.

A person's brain can be easily hurt or injured. A brain injury can happen in different ways, like when a person falls off their bike and hits their head on something. You should always wear a helmet to protect your head when you ride a bike or a skateboard, or play a rough sport like football or hockey.

Brain injuries happen in lots of other ways, too. Sometimes they happen when a person's body is bounced around too hard, when a person gets sick, or after an operation. The worst kind of brain injury is called a traumatic brain injury, or a "TBI" for short. A TBI is an injury to a person's brain that changes how that person thinks, acts, moves or talks.

Sometimes it is hard to know when a person's brain is injured. We cannot see the brain inside their head and they might look and act the same as they always did. The brain doesn't heal like a cut on your finger. A person's brain can stay injured for a long time, sometimes for the person's whole life.

People are different because their brains are different. Two people who have a brain injury will not act the same and their brains will not heal the same way. Each person with a brain injury has to learn to live with the way their injury has changed them.

Family, friends, doctors, nurses, clinicians, and counselors all can support and help a person with a brain injury learn how to feel better about themselves and be happy in their daily life.

How This Book Was Created

I Know You Won't Forget was created, written, and illustrated by survivors of traumatic brain injury in order to provide children with a greater understanding of how parents may be affected by head injury. In the story, a mother with a TBI and her young son learn to work together to develop strategies to overcome her impairments, ultimately finding happiness.

This book is the product of a project-oriented intervention which has continued for more than five years. For members of the group, the project provided a meaningful context for the pursuit of rehabilitation goals following their traumatic brain injuries. While working on the book, the survivors received valuable opportunities to establish meaningful post-injury roles and relationships while working together to help others. Just like the characters in the story, the members of the group collaborated to develop the strategies they needed to overcome their own impairments. Through the use of these strategies and the application of their strengths and personal experiences, these survivors of TBI have brought the story of Joey and his mom to life.

**Truly
Blessed
Ink**

Photo by Michael Cognetti

About the Authors

This book was written by survivors of traumatic brain injury participating in the New York State Department of Health/Medicaid Traumatic Brain Injury Waiver program. They receive support in their homes and communities throughout New York's Capital Region as they pursue their individual goals. In 2003, they established their first weekly group, "Brainstormers," through Crotched Mountain Community Partnership. In 2007, the authors chose to participate in a self-directed group program through Living Resources. Together they provide and receive peer support, plan and participate in social activities, and create projects designed to help others and raise awareness of TBI. Today, they have established ten different groups, and several more groups are being developed. More than 30 survivors have contributed to the creation of this book under the pseudonym, "Truly Blessed Ink." Some group members appear above.

About the Illustrator

Carol Jordan is a wife, mother and grandmother who owns and operates a small arts and crafts studio in Amsterdam, New York. She holds classes almost daily for individuals with disabilities, many of whom are supported by programs through Liberty Enterprises, an ARC agency. In 2003, Carol acquired a brain injury following surgery to remove an acoustic neuroma. She now suffers from total hearing loss in her left ear, mild facial paralysis, and difficulties with balance. As someone who has enjoyed drawing and painting her entire life, Carol believes that art is an effective way to bring out the feelings hidden deep inside us all. She hopes that through her illustrations of the story of Joey and his mom, the family members and friends of TBI survivors will better understand the ways they can help their loved ones. Carol is pictured in her studio.

Photo by Richard Vang

Truly
Blessed
Ink

The "Truly Blessed Ink" Creed

This affirmation is read by a member of "Truly Blessed Ink" before each group meeting:

I am here today to socialize, to work on projects to help others, and to participate in providing and receiving peer support.

I am here to better myself and to practice the skills I have chosen to work on.

I will be accepted for who I am and for my shortcomings. I am open to feedback, good or bad, as long as it is provided respectfully.

I will utilize my strengths to benefit the group, and I promise to be respectful of others and tolerant of their disabilities.

Information About Traumatic Brain Injury

Traumatic Brain Injury (TBI) does not only happen through sudden accidents like a fall from a bike or a hard blow to the head. It can also be the result of a stroke, a brain aneurism, or any circumstance that causes the brain to lose oxygen. It can happen to anyone.

Of the estimated 1.4 million people in the US diagnosed with a TBI each year*, many spend their lives in the shadows of their brain injury because their disabilities are not visible to or understood by others. Many lose their natural abilities and have a difficult time liking the person they have become. However, with a little change of pace, some positive actions, and admitting that change is not something to fear, TBI survivors can live a full and active life.

The organizations listed below offer resources or activities for those affected by a TBI and can help them regain acceptance and assurance in their lives.

International Brain Injury Association
Web site: www.internationalbrain.org

Brain Injury Association of America
Web site: www.biausa.org

Defense and Veterans Brain Injury Center
Web site: www.dvbic.org
Web site: www.brainline.org

Centers for Disease Control and Prevention
Web site: www.cdc.gov/TraumaticBrainInjury/index.html

National Institutes of Health
Web site: www.nlm.nih.gov/medlineplus/traumaticbraininjury.html

The Journey Home - the CEMM Traumatic Brain Injury (TBI) Web Site
Web site: www.traumaticbraininjuryatoz.org

Brain Injury Stories
Web site: www.braininjurystories.org

*Source: Brain Injury Association of America.

Acknowledgments

Truly Blessed Ink would like to thank the following organizations for their continued support of this book project, its publication and its distribution.

Living Resources Foundation

Motivated to provide opportunities for full community integration for all persons with developmental disabilities, a group of caring professionals and parents established Living Resources in 1974. In the mid 1990's, responding to the lack of services for individuals with traumatic or acquired brain injuries, Living Resources joined with Neuro-Psychologic Rehabilitation Services to create a therapeutic model that addressed the cognitive deficits that occur with brain injuries. A holistic, integrated system of activities and psychotherapy aimed at increasing independence and improving self-esteem was developed; this specialized area of services became know as the Acquired Brain Injury (ABI) Department. In addition to hosting the program and providing creative space for Truly Blessed Ink, Living Resources contributed financially to the hardcover first edition of this book.

www.livingresources.org

Brain Injury Association of New York State

Since 1982, the Brain Injury Association of New York State has provided information, resources, advocacy, and support to brain injury survivors, family members, professionals, and educators. BIANYS has further encouraged the members of Truly Blessed Ink by inviting them to speak about the project at conferences, and has been instrumental in promoting the book as an informational resource to its constituents.

www.bianys.org

CPSIA information can be obtained at www.ICGtesting.com
Printed in the USA
BVOW102113110113

310350BV00003B/4/P

9 780985 692629